Exploring Solutions

ONLINE DISINFORMATION AND MISINFORMATION

Carla Mooney

San Diego, CA

Printed in the United States

For more information, contact:
ReferencePoint Press, Inc.
PO Box 27779
San Diego, CA 92198
www.ReferencePointPress.com

LIBRARY OF CONGRESS CATALOGING-IN-PUBLICATION DATA

Names: Mooney, Carla, 1970- author.
Title: Exploring solutions : online disinformation and misinformation / by Carla Mooney.
Description: San Diego, CA : ReferencePoint Press, Inc., 2023. | Series: Exploring solutions | Includes bibliographical references and index.
Identifiers: LCCN 2022056477 (print) | LCCN 2022056478 (ebook) | ISBN 9781678205508 (library binding) | ISBN 9781678205515 (ebook)
Subjects: LCSH: Information technology--Moral and ethical aspects--Juvenile literature. | Disinformation--Juvenile literature. | Misinformation--Juvenile literature. | Truthfulness and falsehood--Juvenile literature.
Classification: LCC ZA3073 .M66 2023 (print) | LCC ZA3073 (ebook) | DDC 303.48/33--dc23/eng/20230106
LC record available at https://lccn.loc.gov/2022056477
LC ebook record available at https://lccn.loc.gov/2022056478

CONTENTS

Misinformation Goes Viral

In October 2022 Dr. Nicole Saphier, a Memorial Sloan Kettering Cancer Center physician, tweeted that the Centers for Disease Control and Prevention (CDC) was about to require all children to get the COVID-19 vaccine in order to attend public school. People read her tweet and shared it with their friends and followers. Within hours, millions of people online had read Saphier's tweet. By that night, a popular cable news show picked up the tweet and talked about it on air. "The CDC is about to add the Covid vaccine to the childhood immunization schedule, which would make the vax mandatory for kids to attend school,"[1] tweeted Fox News host Tucker Carlson. Carlson attached a clip from his show to his tweet and shared it with millions of his followers online.

Action and Reaction

Yet Saphier and Carlson were wrong about the CDC and the COVID-19 vaccine. The CDC does not mandate vaccines for schoolchildren. Instead, individual states and local communities decide which vaccines are mandatory. In reality, the CDC voted to add the COVID-19 vaccine to the federal Vaccines for Children program, which offers free shots to qualifying children.

At first, the CDC did not respond to the false claims about the COVID-19 vaccine. Federal officials worried that addressing Saphier's tweet would further amplify it and give it more attention. However, by the next day the CDC had changed course and tweeted a rebuttal that emphasized the states, not the CDC, determine school vaccine requirements. Yet the CDC's attempt to correct the COVID-19 vaccine misinformation was viewed by many as too late. Public health experts also criticized the CDC's response as confusing because it did not directly reject Carlson's claim and did not use easy-to-understand language. Federal officials worried that the CDC, which quoted Carlson's tweet, had unintentionally amplified the misinformation and spread it to even more people.

Within one day Saphier's original tweet had been shared more than twenty-four hundred times. Public health experts became increasingly concerned about the effects this fast-spreading misinformation would have on people's attitudes toward vaccines and federal health officials. Vaccine critics jumped on the false claim about a COVID-19 mandate for schoolchildren, and outrage toward federal health officials soared. "This is an all new

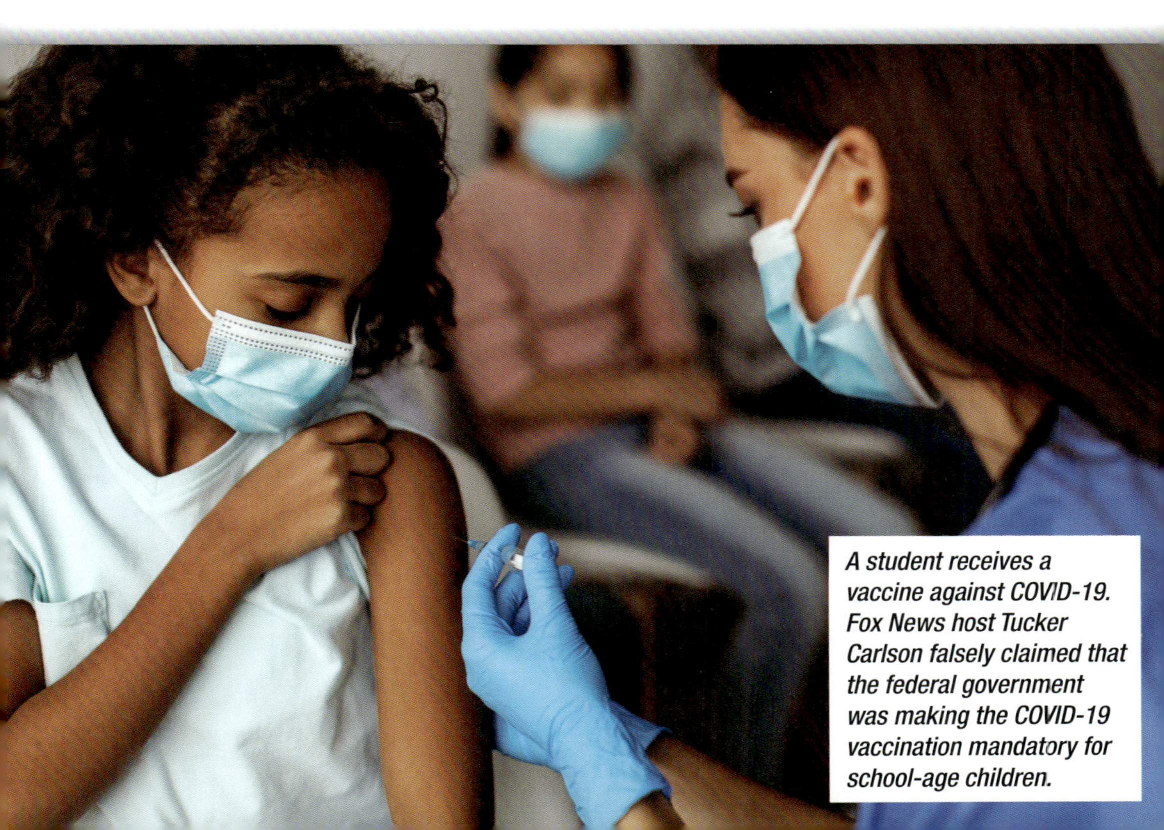

A student receives a vaccine against COVID-19. Fox News host Tucker Carlson falsely claimed that the federal government was making the COVID-19 vaccination mandatory for school-age children.

level of dangerous misinformation," wrote Jerome Adams, a former US surgeon general, in a text message to the *Washington Post*. "It could both harm kids (by derailing the VFC program, which helps disadvantaged children access vaccines) and endanger health officials (due to angry misinformed parents). We need to be able to have honest conversations about pros and cons of vaccinating children, without resorting to blatant misinformation."[2]

In Search of Solutions

Misinformation can spread like wildfire online, reaching people worldwide. Misinformation on topics such as COVID-19 vaccines, the 2021 US Capitol riot, election interference, and more circulate on social media platforms, websites, blogs, and other online sites. And the consequences of misinformation are becoming increasingly serious as more people read and believe the false claims they see online. Misinformation is driving increasing political polarization, endangering public health and communities, and increasing public distrust of the media, government, and other institutions. People are left unsure of what to believe and whom to trust.

The technologies that have drastically improved how everyday people communicate with others worldwide—the internet and social media—have also made the problems of misinformation and disinformation exponentially more challenging to solve. Human nature encourages people to share information, and technology has enabled them to share anything with millions worldwide with a few clicks before the information can truly be verified.

> "Thanks to social media, misinformation and disinformation can spread so much more quickly now. There's no quick fix for this."[3]
>
> —Julie Morita, Chicago's former public health commissioner

The speed with which online information spreads makes trying to stop misinformation and disinformation like trying to chase an elusive and constantly changing target. "I've been doing vaccine work for more than two decades. And what I've seen, thanks to social media, misinformation and disinformation can spread so much more quickly now," says Julie Morita, Chicago's former public health commissioner. "There's no quick fix for this."[3]

Finding a solution is also complicated by concerns about free speech and assigning responsibility for stopping the spread of false information online. Journalist Katie Couric says:

> "Everyone who has a digital device can spread misinformation. And so it's something that we need to pay attention to."[4]
>
> —Katie Couric, journalist

> The sticky wicket in America is free speech. And how do you balance free speech with the need to have outright lies be removed where, unfortunately, an audience is receptive to believing them? I think the technology has almost outrun the ethical considerations of all this. Everyone who has a digital device can spread misinformation. And so it's something that we need to pay attention to.[4]

CHAPTER ONE

The Problem of Online Disinformation and Misinformation

Misinformation and disinformation are everywhere online—and anyone can be deceived, no matter how careful they are. Many people have shared an article or post on social media that they believe is true, and when they discover the information is actually false or out of date, it is too late. It has spread widely online to more people worldwide.

Misinformation vs. Disinformation

Misinformation and disinformation are types of false or misleading information that can deceive those who see them. Both can spread widely online, and the people spreading them may not be aware that the information is false. The main difference between the two is the intention, whether or not the false information was created and spread deliberately.

Misinformation is false, misleading, or out-of-context information that is often spread widely without the intent to mislead. When individuals share a misleading health claim or political conspiracy theory on Facebook, they might believe they are passing on valid information to others who may be interested. Instead, they are spreading misinformation.

An example of misinformation involves claims that 5G cellular networks cause cancer, COVID-19, and other illnesses. 5G is a fast wireless technology that has been implemented in many places worldwide. Health experts have repeatedly explained that the claim is false and 5G radio waves do not make people sick. "This story about 5G has no credence scientifically and is certainly a potential distraction,"[5] says Dr. Jonathan M. Samet, dean of the Colorado School of Public Health.

Even so, people continue to spread this misinformation. In April 2020, for instance, singer Keri Hilson tweeted to her 4.2 million followers, "People have been trying to warn us about 5G for YEARS. Petitions, organizations, studies . . . what we're

Technicians work to install 5G wireless technology on a cell tower in Detroit, Michigan. Health experts have repeatedly tried to counter false claims that 5G radio waves make people sick.

going thru is the effects of radiation. 5G launched in CHINA. Nov 1, 2019. People dropped dead."[6] These claims are false; they are unsupported by evidence. Yet they continue to make the rounds on social media.

Disinformation Is Designed to Deceive

People who spread misinformation do not necessarily intend to mislead others. This is different from disinformation, which is purposely created and deliberately spread to deceive. The main objectives of those who create and spread disinformation are political power, profit, or sowing public chaos and confusion. Disinformation is an effective tool in times of uncertainty or when public distrust of institutions is high. "When you've got a lack of correct information and an anxious population with a lot at stake, disinformation is going to flourish. When people are anxious and looking for answers, somebody is going to provide those answers and capitalize on it financially or politically,"[7] says Brian Southwell, a director at RTI International, a nonprofit research institute.

In 2022 Russia used disinformation as a weapon in its war against Ukraine. When Ukraine reported that Russian forces were killing civilians, Russia spread a video claiming the Ukrainians had dressed up mannequins as dead bodies and that their reports of casualties were false. Several websites and social media accounts have pushed other pro-Russian disinformation related to the war. Claims include allegations that Ukraine staged the Russian attacks to generate global sympathy, Ukrainian president Volodymyr Zelenskyy faked his public appearances, and refugees from Ukraine committed crimes in Poland and Germany. "These campaigns serve to create divisions, sow distrust, and pivot the conversation to other issues that cloud judgment and weaken the collective response of Ukrainian allies,"[8] writes Aloysius Uche Ordu, a senior fellow at the Brookings Institution, a nonprofit public policy organization.

> "When you've got a lack of correct information and an anxious population with a lot at stake, disinformation is going to flourish."[7]
>
> —Brian Southwell, a director at RTI International, a nonprofit research institute

Workers in Bucha, Ukraine, exhume bodies of people killed by Russian troops in 2022. Several websites and social media accounts have spread pro-Russian disinformation claiming that Ukraine dressed up mannequins as dead bodies and that claims of civilian casualties are false.

Efforts have been made to block disinformation, but creators often manage to get around those restrictions. This happened after the European Union and several tech companies banned Russia's state-run media from their platforms for spreading disinformation videos. To disguise their source, the Russian creators of the fake videos removed identifying marks and then uploaded the videos to the messaging app Telegram. Telegram users reposted the videos on other social media platforms, including Twitter. Then hundreds of accounts linked to the Russian state media, military, or embassies posted or reposted the videos across social media, allowing the Russian disinformation to slip past the ban. "The genius of this approach is that the videos can be downloaded directly from Telegram and it erases the trail that researchers try to follow. They are creative and adaptable,"[9] says Patricia Bailey, a senior intelligence analyst with cyber intelligence firm Nisos.

Going Viral Online

False and misleading information thrives online, thanks in large part to the enormous number of people worldwide who use the internet and social media. "The scale of reach that you have with social media, and the speed at which it spreads, is really like nothing humanity has ever seen,"[10] says Jevin West, a disinformation researcher at the University of Washington.

Before the internet, news organizations acted as gatekeepers to verify the information printed in newspapers or aired on television news programs. Now on the internet, anyone can create a website, start a blog, or post on social media. These communication technologies provide a low-cost, low-barrier way to spread information globally with a few clicks. Naveena Srinivas, an information technology analyst, says, "The speed and the volume of data shared via advancing technologies continue to widen the potential impact of misinformation in news coverage. Whether it's about climate change, US elections, the Omicron variant, or COVID-19 vaccine information updates, misinformation continues to spread like wildfire across the internet."[11]

The bogus Bill Gates microchip story is one example of how quickly misinformation can spread online. On March 18, 2020, Microsoft founder Bill Gates posted in an online forum that using electronic records instead of paper forms might be an easier way to track who had received the COVID-19 vaccine. Almost immediately, other forum users began to post comments about implantable microchips, even though Gates never mentioned them in his original post. The next day a website posted an article claiming that Gates wanted to implant electronic devices into people to record their vaccine history. A day later a YouTube video took it further, claiming that Gates wanted to track people's movements. The conspiracy theory circulated and picked up steam, with people convinced that Gates was using the COVID-19 vaccine to implant microchips into people to track their movements. The conspiracy theory even jumped to newspa-

"Whether it's about climate change, US elections, the Omicron variant, or COVID-19 vaccine information updates, misinformation continues to spread like wildfire across the internet."[11]

—Naveena Srinivas, an information technology analyst

Deepfake Technology

Deepfake technology can make fake content even more difficult to spot. Deepfakes are audio, video, or images that use artificial intelligence to replace a person's likeness with that of another in a very realistic way. Synthesized speech technology can match the voice of a person and create statements or words he or she never said. Deepfakes are created to trick users into believing a fake event or false message. Users who are taken in by deepfakes often share them. And then others share them as well, and this continues to the point that thousands or even millions of people end up seeing the fake (and usually provocative) content.

This happened in 2019, when a deepfake video of Speaker of the House Nancy Pelosi circulated on Facebook. In the video, Pelosi appeared to be drunk, impaired, or ill. Although the video was fabricated, within a week it had attracted nearly 3 million views and was shared more than 48,000 times.

per and cable news platforms like the *New York Post* and Fox News. Even though fact-checking organizations and reputable journalists have repeatedly reported the claim as false, it still circulates online. In May 2020 a Yahoo News/YouGov poll found that 44 percent of Republicans and 19 percent of Democrats believed the story to be true.

Misinformation often contains a kernel of truth, which helps make those stories more believable. For example, a 2019 paper published by Massachusetts Institute of Technology (MIT) researchers provided that kernel for the false Gates microchip story. In that paper, the researchers described a tattoo ink made from tiny semiconductor particles. A tattoo done with this ink could contain a person's vaccination history, and that information could be accessed by a specially designed smartphone. This research, funded by the Gates Foundation, is still in early stages of development and far from human testing. Within a short time, however, it was transformed into the bogus story that circulated over the internet. "It isn't outlandish. It's just outlandish to say it will then be used by Gates in some sinister way,"[12] says Neil Johnson, a physicist at George Washington University who studies misinformation.

Who Spreads Misinformation and Disinformation?

Research shows that most misinformation is spread by a relatively small number of social media users. A 2019 study of Twitter, for instance, found that 80 percent of misinformation related to the 2016 US presidential election came from only 0.1 percent of its users. That misinformation was further amplified by politicians and others—known as super-spreaders—who have access to millions of people across social media and other online sites.

Human users are not entirely to blame for the spread of false information on social media. When false information spreads quickly and widely, bots are likely involved. Bots are automated programs designed to behave like human social media users. While some bots are harmless, many are deployed specifically for the purpose of spreading rumors, disinformation, and other inflammatory content.

Researchers at Carnegie Mellon University reviewed more than 200 million pandemic-related tweets in 2020. Nearly half (45 percent) of the Twitter accounts spreading messages about the COVID-19 pandemic appeared to come from bots rather than from individual users. The researchers identified more than one hundred false claims about COVID-19 being spread by bot-controlled Twitter accounts. While the researchers could not identify the people or organizations behind the tweets, they believe the messages were sent to create division among Americans.

Reputable News Sources Harder to Determine Online

Misinformation and disinformation are a growing problem partly because of a fundamental change in how people get their news. Before social media and the internet, established news organizations and journalists provided news to the general public through newspapers, radio, and television. These traditional avenues made it easy to determine whether a news source was reputable.

New Social Platforms

The fight against misinformation and disinformation has mainly focused on major social media platforms such as Twitter and Facebook. However, in recent years dozens of new platforms have emerged, many of which have few policies on moderating or removing false content. While these platforms are small, misinformation and disinformation, if left unchecked, can easily jump from one to another, eventually landing on major platforms and even mainstream media sites.

In July 2021, for example, former president Donald Trump shared on Truth Social, a social media platform he founded, the false claim that he had won the 2020 presidential vote in Wisconsin. Truth Social is a small social media platform, and only eight thousand users shared Trump's post. However, the false claim quickly leaped from Truth Social to other social media platforms, podcasts, talk radio programs, and television broadcasts. Within forty-eight hours of Trump's post, more than 1 million people had viewed it on at least a dozen sites, including major social media platforms like Facebook and Twitter. "Nothing on the internet exists in a silo. Whatever happens in alt platforms like Gab or Telegram or Truth makes its way back to Facebook and Twitter and others," says Jared Holt, a senior manager on hate and extremism research at the Institute for Strategic Dialogue.

Quoted in Steven Lee Myers and Sheera Frenkel, "How Disinformation Splintered and Became More Intractable," *New York Times*, October 20, 2022. www.nytimes.com.

Since the introduction of the internet and social media platforms, more Americans are going online to get their news. Whether using Google, Twitter, Facebook, or media websites, checking for news online has become common. Smartphone alerts and mobile apps bring the latest news to people more quickly than ever. In 2022, 82 percent of American adults said they often or sometimes got their news from a smartphone, computer, or tablet, according to a survey by the Pew Research Center.

When online, many Americans get their news from social media platforms. While social media distributes news stories from reputable media sources, these stories appear in news feeds along with a mix of other content. Fact-based news stories from known, reputable sources appear next to content from questionable sources. And when social media sites use algorithms to tailor a user's feed to his or her specific interests, a person may not see reputable news stories that provide other perspectives. The way social media feeds give content from different sources a similar look makes it more difficult for users to determine whether a source is reputable or whether information is true or false. As a result, it becomes easier for false information to take hold and spread.

Confusing Fact and Fiction

People who spend hours scrolling through social media may not fully understand the pitfalls of reading news on these platforms. Headlines and posts on social media sites are often designed to be inflammatory to increase user engagement in the form of likes and comments. Many people consume this content online without evaluating the accuracy of what they see. US adults who rely on social media for major news stories are less knowledgeable about news topics than those who get their news elsewhere, according to a 2020 Pew Research Center analysis.

Additionally, people who get their news on social media are more likely to see misinformation and disinformation. The same Pew Research Center analysis found that 81 percent of US adults who primarily rely on social media for news reported that they had heard about a conspiracy theory that the COVID-19 pandemic was intentionally planned. In comparison, adults who relied on other sources of news were less likely to have heard this false theory.

Spotting a bogus story can be challenging even for people who are careful about what they read on social media. The format of social media sites contributes to the confusion, according to a 2020 study by researchers at Ohio State University. When people get news, political information, funny memes, and pictures from the same place, it becomes more challenging to recognize fact from fiction. Satire and fiction can more easily be mistaken for real news. "We are drawn to these social media sites because they are one-stop shops for media content, updates from friends and family, and memes or cat pictures," says George Pearson, a research associate at Ohio State University and author of the study.

"But that jumbling of content makes everything seem the same to us. It makes it harder for us to distinguish what we need to take seriously from that which is only entertainment."[13]

Also, many social media platforms present content similarly, regardless of the source. A *New York Times* Facebook post might, for instance, have the same font and color scheme as a post from a personal blog. Although they are completely different sources, they look identical. A user could not tell them apart with just a casual glance. In fact, 86 percent of internet users admit they have fallen for fake news, most of it spread on social media, according to a 2019 global survey by the Centre for International Governance Innovation.

> "We are drawn to these social media sites because they are one-stop shops for media content, updates from friends and family, and memes or cat pictures. But that jumbling of content makes everything seem the same to us. It makes it harder for us to distinguish what we need to take seriously from that which is only entertainment."[13]
>
> —George Pearson, a research associate at Ohio State University

How Serious Is the Problem?

Misinformation and disinformation can have serious consequences. In a nationwide 2022 poll by the University of Chicago Pearson Institute/AP-NORC, 91 percent of American adults agree that misinformation is a growing problem. About 70 percent believe misinformation contributes to extreme political views and hate crimes motivated by gender, race, or religion. About half of the respondents said that misinformation was also causing a decline in public trust of government.

Americans are also concerned by the impact of misinformation and disinformation on American democracy. In another 2022 poll by National Public Radio, 64 percent of respondents said they believed that US democracy was in crisis and at risk of failing. Many believe that disinformation designed to create doubt around US elections and disrupt the democratic process is to blame.

Disinformation and misinformation are also driving public confidence in the mainstream media to new lows. A July 2022 Gallup poll revealed that Americans' confidence in newspapers and television news had dropped to the lowest recorded levels. In the poll, only 16 percent of respondents said they had a great deal or a lot of confidence in newspapers, while only 11 percent had some degree of confidence in television news. In a 2020 study, researchers from Northeastern University and Rutgers University found that participants exposed to misinformation over one month experienced a 5 percent decrease in media trust. "Fake news sources often target mainstream media organizations by accusing them of bias and incompetence," the researchers write. "Perhaps more importantly, sensational and made-up stories that mimic the format of journalism could damage the credibility of all news content."[14]

Misinformation and disinformation can also damage a company's or brand's reputation. False information that generates headlines can cause sales and stock prices to drop and cause affected companies to spend significant amounts of time and money on repairing their reputation. In 2022 a fake Twitter account claiming to be the pharmaceutical company Eli Lilly tweeted an announce-

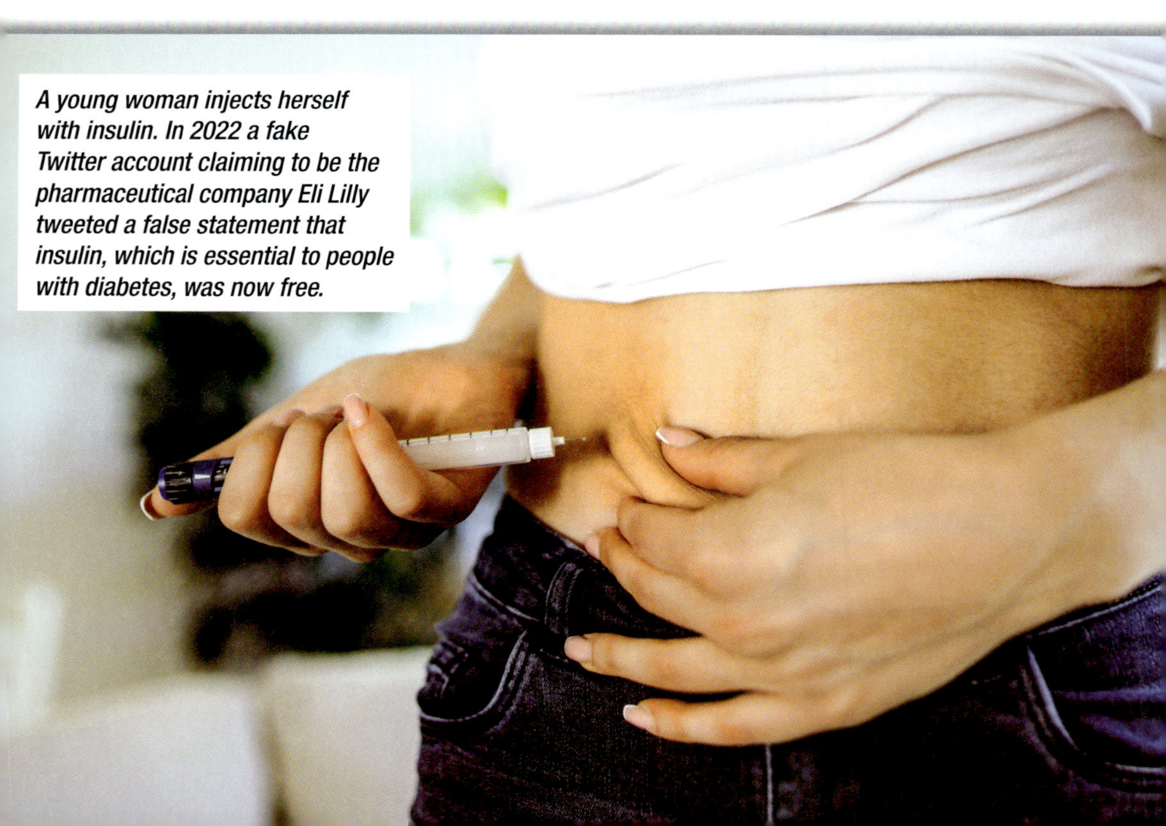

A young woman injects herself with insulin. In 2022 a fake Twitter account claiming to be the pharmaceutical company Eli Lilly tweeted a false statement that insulin, which is essential to people with diabetes, was now free.

ment that insulin—essential to people with diabetes—was now free. The fake account looked a lot like the company's real Twitter account. Within hours, the fake tweet gathered ten thousand likes and thousands of retweets. The company, which is one of the premier makers of insulin, quickly issued a statement on its official Twitter account to correct the false tweet. However, the damage had already been done. Within a few hours, the company's stock dropped 4.5 percent, wiping out billions of dollars of the company's value.

Potential Solutions to a Complex Problem

While many agree that misinformation and disinformation are a problem that needs to be addressed, there is debate over potential solutions. Some people believe that a technology-based solution will be the most effective, while others support additional laws and regulations to prevent the spread of misinformation online. Other approaches focus on improving media literacy and educating people on how to recognize misinformation when they encounter it online. Some of these ideas will be harder to accomplish than others.

Misinformation will never go away. But a combination of solutions may help slow it down and diminish its effects. "It's more of a problem to be managed like a chronic disease," says Renee DiResta, a disinformation researcher at the Stanford Internet Observatory. "It's not something you're going to cure."[15]

CHAPTER TWO

Using Technology to Detect Misinformation and Disinformation

Technology has enabled misinformation and disinformation to spread worldwide over the internet and social media. Gary Fowler, an artificial intelligence (AI) entrepreneur, says:

> We live in a reality that's all the more influenced by the hyperconnectivity and constant interactions we now experience in the real and digital worlds alike. The rise of fake news in the last decade can be largely attributed to that exact factor—the ease with which digital content can be created, distributed and consumed through a variety of digital platforms, from social media to websites and private messengers.[16]

Technology may also be a solution to help detect and stop false information before it spreads. Currently, social media platforms and online sites use human content-moderators and fact-checkers to sift through content. Their role is to determine whether content posted on the site meets the platform's community guidelines, which are aimed at creating a safe place for users to interact. If the content does not, platforms can remove it, label it as unreliable, or even suspend or ban untrustworthy accounts. For example, Facebook pays independent fact-checking organizations to review content and rate its accuracy. For content rated false, Facebook labels the content as such and moves it lower in its feed algorithm so fewer people will see it. However, the sheer volume of content online makes it next to impossible for these organizations to identify and fact-check a significant enough amount of misinformation and disinformation.

Technology solutions that can automate these processes could be a critical part of slowing the spread of false information online. Because repeated exposure to the same information increases the chances a person will believe it, reducing how much misinformation appears can break the cycle and slow its spread. "While this issue has proliferated due to the technological

Facebook pays independent fact-checking organizations to review content and rate its accuracy. Facebook labels content that is rated false and takes steps to reduce the number of people who see it.

advancements that the digital transformation has spurred, it also means that technological advancements will be the solution to this increasingly dangerous issue,"[17] says Fowler.

However, technology is not a quick fix for this problem. Financial, logistical, and legal concerns stand in the way. It is possible that some of these concerns can be overcome, but some present difficult choices. Either way, many people believe that technology alone cannot fix the problem of misinformation and disinformation.

Using Artificial Intelligence

Artificial intelligence (AI) is a promising tool in the fight against misinformation and disinformation. AI is an area of computer science that involves building smart machines and software programs to perform tasks that typically require human intelligence. AI technology teaches computers to automatically perform specific tasks by training them on massive data sets. With AI, computers can process and fact-check large volumes of information quickly. According to Fowler:

> Artificial intelligence is among the best options designed to supplement our efforts as humans in the fight for the truth and against misinformation. With its ability to train on data samples of various sizes and quickly learn the ability to discern patterns, identify anomalies and predict events in the future, artificial intelligence is perfectly positioned to become an ideal tool for fighting propaganda and minimizing the risk of viral fake information.[18]

"Artificial intelligence is among the best options designed to supplement our efforts as humans in the fight for the truth and against misinformation."[18]

—Gary Fowler, an artificial intelligence entrepreneur

AI can be used in different ways to detect misinformation and disinformation. Some companies are developing natural language processing (NLP) algorithms. NLP can teach an algorithm to classify text as true or false by training it on large amounts of data manually marked as true

Defining Disinformation

Microsoft Corporation, which owns the LinkedIn social network and the Bing search engine, says that it will not label social media posts as false because the company does not want to appear to be censoring online speech. In an interview with Bloomberg News, Microsoft president Brad Smith explained, "I don't think that people want governments to tell them what's true or false. And I don't think they're really interested in having tech companies tell them either."

Instead, Microsoft has invested in information operation analysts and technology tools to track online propaganda campaigns. These analysts work with Microsoft's cybersecurity team to track disinformation campaigns and inform the public about them. The company's primary goal is to be transparent about the efforts it is making to combat disinformation, according to Smith. "Our whole approach needs to be to provide people with more information, not less," he says.

Quoted in Margi Murphy, "Microsoft Won't Label Fake News as False in an Attempt to Avoid 'Censorship' Cries," Bloomberg News, September 21, 2022. www.bloomberg.com.

or false. NLP can also match text against information held in a large database that has been fact-checked.

AI can also use pattern recognition to identify misinformation and disinformation. Instead of trying to classify information as true or false, this type of AI trains an algorithm to analyze patterns and spot online accounts that appear to be bots or to have come from troll farms or click farms. Troll farms are groups of users paid to spread propaganda and unrest online. Click farms pay people to click on content and ads to make them appear more popular online. Like bots, both can be indicators of disinformation. Jennifer Granston, the chief customer officer at the intelligence software service company Zignal Labs, explains how her company's pattern-recognition AI works. "We don't label content as 'true or false' or 'harmful or not harmful.' NLP and different . . . models allow us to identify, for example, what accounts on Twitter behave as if they are using a high level of automation—or which accounts are likely to be bots, click farms or troll farms—the ones propagating bad content,"[19] she says.

Fact-checking is another area that could benefit from artificial intelligence. Human fact-checkers simply cannot keep up with the amount of content—and misinformation—on social media. A UK start-up company called Logically has developed an AI program for verifying the accuracy of news, social discussion, and images. Logically uses AI algorithms to understand and analyze text and check content, metadata, and images. The AI software labels the credibility of each source with a rating of high, medium, or low. It also marks articles as reliable or unreliable based on comparisons with similar content. Users can download a free app and verify content by sharing it with Logically. Users can also fact-check stories with a Chrome browser extension that works on more than 160,000 social media platforms and news sites. During a recent election cycle in India, Logically analyzed more than 1 million articles and uncovered 50,000 that contained false information.

Women line up to cast votes in a 2018 election in India. During the election cycle, an artificial intelligence application was used to identify news articles that contained false information meant to influence voters like these.

Keeping Up with the Speed of Disinformation

Not only can AI help sort through the volume of content online, it can also do it much more quickly than human fact-checkers. When a news story breaks, it appears on multiple outlets and sources with incredible speed. AI could be used to simultaneously check variations of the same news story appearing on different sources and platforms, from social media to blogs and websites. Using AI to cross-reference and compare facts and reporting across platforms could more quickly and efficiently identify errors and misinformation in content. And the sooner false information is detected, the easier it is to stop its spread.

A group of computer experts at MIT set out to develop an AI technology that could automatically and quickly detect disinformation being spread on social media networks. The project, called Reconnaissance of Influence Operations (RIO), published a paper in 2021 about its results using AI to detect disinformation around the 2017 French elections. In the thirty days before the elections, the team gathered 28 million Twitter posts from 1 million accounts. Then the team used the RIO system to detect and analyze the social media posts for disinformation. The RIO system was able to quickly detect disinformation with 96 percent accuracy. The RIO system can create a comprehensive picture of where and how disinformation spreads. This allows RIO to identify accounts that are actively spreading disinformation and shut them down quickly before they cause more damage. The team sees RIO being used in the future by government and industry partners and expanding beyond social media into traditional newspapers and television.

The Limits of Technology

Technology can be a powerful tool in the fight against misinformation and disinformation, but it has limits. Artificial intelligence relies on enormous amounts of data, so machines can learn to recognize specific patterns in the data and learn from experience. However, for AI to accurately identify misinformation, the data models used for training must be built with unbiased and representative data sets, such as data from different platforms and geographic regions. If not, the AI results can be biased or inaccurate. Also, building a data set suitable for AI training can take a significant amount of time.

Even with adequate data for training, machines may have difficulty detecting the nuances in content. Machines and AI algorithms lack the political, cultural, and social knowledge necessary to identify misinformation. In 2019, for example, YouTube was forced to apologize after an AI tool designed to detect misinformation mistakenly linked the fire at Notre Dame Cathedral in Paris to the Sep-

After fire damaged Notre Dame Cathedral in Paris in 2019, an AI tool designed to detect misinformation mistakenly linked the fire to the September 11, 2001, terrorist attacks in the United States.

tember 11, 2001, terrorist attacks in the United States. The AI tool was intended to fact-check content and slow the spread of conspiracy theories on the platform. This time, however, it incorrectly displayed text from *Encyclopaedia Britannica* about 9/11 with videos of the cathedral in flames. This type of mistake could have been easily caught by a human fact-checker. "AI tools are great at dealing with high quantities of information at fast speeds but lack the nuanced analysis that a journalist or fact-checker can provide. I see a future where the two work together,"[20] says Benjamin D. Horne, an assistant professor of information sciences at the University of Tennessee.

> **"AI tools are great at dealing with high quantities of information at fast speeds but lack the nuanced analysis that a journalist or fact-checker can provide. I see a future where the two work together."[20]**
>
> —Benjamin D. Horne, assistant professor of information sciences at the University of Tennessee

Hiring people to partner with AI technology to verify content can be a solution. In Lithuania the government developed an AI program that works with human specialists to detect and flag misinformation. Lithuanian deputy minister of defense Edvinas Kerza explains, "This artificial intelligence 'eats' all news from all news portals . . . and analyzes the texts, looks for fake news, documents. It takes around two minutes. After that, it passes the analysis to . . . [human] professionals. Based on their assessment, a text can be automatically defined if it is fake or not and then this information goes to news portals."[21]

AI algorithms follow the instructions and parameters of their programming. Sometimes, even a human specialist may have trouble judging whether content is false. Determining who is responsible for deciding what is misinformation is another potential pitfall with AI algorithms. If AI is given faulty instructions or parameters, it may incorrectly classify content.

AI Solutions in the Wrong Hands

While technology companies are working to improve AI algorithms against misinformation and disinformation, some people with less honorable intentions are using the same technology to promote

"Part of the challenge is that AI is an open field. It releases I ts research openly, and that has driven innovation. It's also a double-edged sword because threat actors can leverage that."[22]

—Katerina Sedova, a research fellow at the Center for Security and Emerging Technology at Georgetown University

and spread disinformation online. "Part of the challenge is that AI is an open field. It releases its research openly, and that has driven innovation. It's also a double-edged sword because threat actors can leverage that,"[22] says Katerina Sedova, a research fellow at the Center for Security and Emerging Technology at Georgetown University.

AI can be used in several ways to make disinformation harder to detect and stop. A deepfake is one of the most common forms of AI used for disinformation. Also, web robots or bot accounts, which are often used to post and spread disinformation, can become more human-like using AI, which helps them evade bot detection systems. As technology companies get better at detecting false information, disinformation creators are also getting better at making and spreading it. "Unfortunately, the systems that generate [disinformation] are in a race with the systems that detect them, and they are learning from each other,"[23] says Sedova. As a result of this technology race, the AI solutions developed today may not be able to detect misinformation and disinformation in the future.

Additionally, AI systems have the potential for misuse. For example, authoritarian governments may direct AI systems to remove any content they decide is negative or unflattering. In China the government is already using AI to limit free speech and block content it decides is objectionable. Taking it further, authoritarian governments may use AI systems to identify content creators so they can prosecute them. "AI has facilitated a whole new level of state control over communications infrastructure and the information realm. Its technological advantages include scaled capacity to scan for forbidden content and filter out dissenting views,"[24] says Eileen Donahoe, executive director of Stanford University's Global Digital Policy Incubator. Therefore, AI systems must be transparent to the public and have independent third-party monitoring to be effective.

Is AI a Good Idea?

In recent years the major social media platforms have begun to label content that they determine contains false information. Nearly three-quarters of social media users (74 percent) say they have seen content on social media sites that is labeled or flagged as false, according to a November 2021 Pew Research Center survey. However, Americans are unsure about whether using artificial intelligence to fight false information on social media platforms is a good idea. In the survey, 38 percent of respondents thought it was a good idea, 31 percent said it was a bad idea, and 30 percent were unsure. Many people believe that AI algorithms probably or definitely lead to censoring of political viewpoints (70 percent) and the wrongful removal of news and information from the sites (69 percent). A majority of respondents believe that humans should be involved in the decision to remove content from social media sites and that the site should prioritize accuracy over speed.

Blockchain Technology

Some digital experts believe blockchain technology is another promising solution against misinformation and disinformation. Blockchain is a database technology that allows multiple parties to read and write in a shared database. It tracks changes made in the database in a log called a ledger. Blockchain systems are decentralized, which means they are not controlled by a single person or group, and the ledger is constantly verified each time a party uses it. This constant verification process makes it extremely difficult to change information in the database. Currently, blockchain is used to manage cryptocurrency transactions like Bitcoin. But it may also be an effective way to track all types of online content.

Blockchain could be used against misinformation and disinformation by tracking and verifying sources for online media. For example, organizations could use blockchain to create a registry of published images. Image information such as when and where it was created, why it was made, and a history of how news organizations have used it could be included in the database. As an image or video is uploaded, information about it can be pulled from the blockchain database and placed in a pop-up text next to it. Readers can verify the media, its source, and whether it is being used accurately in a given context.

The *New York Times* is exploring the use of blockchain technology to track image data. "We wanted to see whether visible contextual information, such as the photographer's name and the location depicted in the photo, could help readers better discern the credibility of news photos in their social feeds,"[25] says the newspaper's research and development team. When testing their prototype with users, the *New York Times* team found that it helped users make informed judgments about photos that appear on social media. But the team emphasizes that more research is needed. "This experiment taught us a lot about the power of credible, contextual information in social media feeds, but there is a long way to go before something like this can be fully realized. Nevertheless, there is a large opportunity for using blockchain to help fight against misinformation in news photos,"[26] asserts the team.

As more people get their news from social media feeds or other online sources, it has become more challenging to determine credible sources and journalists. Blockchain technology could also be used to verify online news articles and their authors. A blockchain database could record an article's content and publication data. The changes are logged in the database whenever edits to the article are made. This transparent documentation makes it easy for people to verify the source of a news article and see whether others have manipulated it.

Several media companies have implemented blockchain-based systems to verify the source of their content. In 2020 the Italian news agency ANSA released a blockchain system that allowed readers to verify the origin of news articles published on its platform. ANSA's digital seal confirms that an article is recorded in the blockchain database, which verifies that the article came from ANSA instead of another source. While the ANSA solution does not fact-check the article, it prevents readers from being tricked into thinking false articles came from a reputable source like ANSA. Although this technology will not stop people from posting misinformation and disinformation, the technology could make it easier to identify and slow false information's spread.

Technology to Slow Misinformation's Online Spread

The viral spread of misinformation and disinformation online has been made possible by technological advances like the internet and social media. It is only fitting that technology may also be part of the solution to stop false and misleading content online. Scientists are developing ways to use technologies like artificial intelligence and blockchain technology to detect, identify, and remove misinformation from websites and social media platforms. "As the pursuit of fighting fake news becomes more sophisticated, technology leaders will continue to work to find even better ways to sort out fact from fiction [as] well as refine the AI tools that can help fight disinformation,"[27] says Bernard Marr, a business and technology adviser.

CHAPTER THREE

New Laws and Regulations

Technology has the potential to be an effective way to combat misinformation and disinformation. However, tech companies and social media sites have been slow to utilize these tools effectively. Websites, social media platforms, and other online sites have few incentives to crack down on misinformation and disinformation. Therefore, many people believe that the only way to solve the problem is for governments to pass laws and regulations that require these companies to take the issue seriously and protect citizens.

Engaging Content Makes Money

Social media platforms and other online sites primarily make money by selling advertising on their sites. This idea is not new; it has been used for years in traditional media like newspapers, radio, and television. Companies pay for advertising spots to get their ads in front of consumers watching a television program, reading a newspaper, or interacting on social media. On websites and social media platforms, companies buy ads that are placed throughout the site or platform. Sites with the most users are most attractive to advertisers since they can reach more potential customers. The more users on a site, the more advertisers want to be on it, and the more they will be willing to pay for ads.

Therefore, websites and social media platforms have a strong incentive to attract users to their sites. The more users they have, the more money they can make from advertising. To do this, they promote engaging content that users want to read, view, and interact with through likes, comments, and shares. Social media platforms develop algorithms to help them promote engaging content and attract users. The algorithms do this by sorting through content and prioritizing posts in users' feeds. The algorithms attempt to put content higher in users' feeds based on the likelihood that they will want to see it. In this way the platforms try to attract and engage users by giving them a steady stream of posts they find interesting and engaging.

The social media posts that perform the best and generate the most engagement are also some of the most controversial. Research has shown that content that is politically inflammatory or includes moral outrage is more likely to have greater user engagement and spread faster. Many of these controversial posts contain false or misleading information.

For example, a 2020 analysis by the nonprofit news organizations ProPublica and First Draft showed that high-engagement content about elections and voting by mail on social media sites like Facebook included many false or misleading posts. Of the fifty most popular posts about voting by mail, the analysis found, 44 percent included misinformation. Although many of the false claims in those posts appeared to violate Facebook's content standards, they remained on the platform for people to read and share. Most were not removed or marked as inaccurate until ProPublica and First Draft publicly identified them. However, for many, Facebook's actions were too little, too late. "It was all talk, no action. We hear words like 'We know we need to do better' and 'We're working on this,' and yet misinformation still seems to be quite pervasive on the site,"[28] says Jessica González, the co–chief executive officer (CEO) of Free Press, an advocacy group focused on media and technology.

Websites and social media platforms attract users to their sites by promoting engaging content that users want to view, read, and interact with.

Slow Progress, Competing Interests

Critics say social media companies and other online sites have many options available to stop the spread of false information on their sites. They could use stricter procedures to verify content creators' identities to ensure creators are who they claim to be. Google is already doing this for its advertisers, and Facebook has a voluntary verification process for accounts. However, verification is not required, and most Facebook accounts remain unverified. Websites and social media platforms could also invest in technology solutions to screen content and users for misinformation and disinformation.

However, the sites have been slow to address the problem. "If you look at Facebook and Twitter—the platforms themselves—they know to a certain extent that these things were occurring. It's just that they have different motivations," says Hatim Rahman, an assistant professor of management and organizations at the Kellogg School of Management at Northwestern University. Rahman explains that ignoring misinformation may be beneficial for these sites. "Viral content pays. It attracts more advertisement, more eyeballs, more time and attention to the platforms. But we've seen serious trade-offs to maximizing those types of metrics for platforms,"[29] says Rahman.

Platform Content Policies

Currently, the most popular social media platforms and websites have similar policies for deciding what content to allow on their sites. They ban posts that encourage violence or are sexually explicit. They also ban hate speech, which is defined as a post that attacks a person for race, gender, sexual orientation, or other characteristics. These platforms have started fact-checking posts, labeling posts from media controlled by foreign governments, and banning political ads entirely to slow disinformation. These platforms follow the laws of the countries where they operate, which can add additional restrictions.

Policies that fight misinformation by removing or limiting popular false or misleading content can cause user engagement to drop, hitting websites and social media platforms financially. Critics say this reduces efforts by these companies to lead the push for misinformation solutions. Therefore, many believe the government needs to step in and actively regulate social media and other online platforms to slow the spread of misinformation.

Calls for Regulation and Oversight

To date, there are no laws in the United States specifically addressing the internet, social media, and misinformation. In 1996 Congress passed the Communications Decency Act in an attempt to regulate pornography on the internet and prevent children from accessing indecent content. One part of the act, called Section 230, gives broad protections to internet service providers and other online platforms that host or republish content from third parties. Under Section 230, tech companies and social media sites are not liable for most of the content posted on their platforms. Because of these protections, social media sites cannot be held responsible or sued when users upload false information or other objectionable content to their sites.

In March 2021 members of the US House of Representatives held a hearing to explore issues related to social media and misinformation and look at how regulation and government oversight could be a solution. Lawmakers questioned the CEOs of Facebook, Google, and Twitter about several issues related to misinformation and extremism. Noting the failure of the industry to adequately address misinformation and disinformation, several lawmakers called for increased regulation. In his opening statement, Representative Frank Pallone Jr. stated:

> We are here today because the spread of disinformation and extremism has been growing online, particularly on social media, where there are little to no guardrails in place to stop it. And unfortunately, this disinformation and extremism doesn't just stay online. It has real world, often dangerous and even violent consequences. The time has come to hold online platforms accountable for their part in the rise of disinformation and extremism.[30]

Pallone noted that COVID-19 vaccine hesitation, the January 6 Capitol attack, increasing domestic violent extremism, and rising hate crimes against Asian Americans could all be linked to misinformation and disinformation campaigns online. He said:

> Each of these controversies and crimes have been accelerated and amplified on social media platforms through misinformation campaigns, the spread of hate speech, and the proliferation of conspiracy theories. . . . It is now painfully clear that neither the market nor public pressure will force these social media companies to take the aggressive action they need to take to eliminate disinformation and extremism from their platforms. And, therefore, it is time for Congress and this Committee to legislate and realign these companies' incentives to effectively deal with disinformation and extremism.[31]

Some in government say that incidents such as the January 6, 2021, Capitol attack (shown here) can be linked to misinformation and disinformation campaigns online.

Martha Minow, a professor at Harvard Law School, agrees that social media companies acting alone cannot solve the problem of misinformation and disinformation. Instead, government involvement in the search for a solution is needed. She says:

> The government can act by enforcing, or strengthening and then enforcing, consumer protection rules. . . . The government can act by limiting the immunity granted to internet platforms and condition it on the development of codes of conduct that are then enforced. And the government can act by making rules that require sharing the information about the algorithms and their uses with a watchdog, whether academic or nonprofit organizations. We need to improve the entire ecosystem in which information circulates.[32]

Proposed Laws and Reforms

Some lawmakers favor new laws to regulate social media and other online platforms. Others believe it is time for Congress to

States Try to Prohibit Content Blocking

Lawmakers in more than two dozen US states are attempting to pass new legislation to prevent tech companies from censoring content or blocking users. Two states—Florida and Texas—have signed bills into law. In Florida a 2021 law bans tech companies from removing political candidates from their platforms. In Texas a similar 2021 law bans social media companies from restricting online viewpoints. Supporters of these laws say they protect users' free speech rights. However, the tech companies disagree and argue that the laws infringe on their First Amendment rights to decide what content they will host on their platforms.

As of 2022 federal courts had blocked the Florida and Texas laws from taking effect. Many legal scholars believe that the state governments cannot tell a private company that it must host certain content, and the Florida and Texas laws will eventually be overturned. Others warn that taking a state-by-state approach to regulation of online platforms could create confusion. "You cannot have a state-by-state internet. When you step back and look at the possibility of having 50 different state laws on content moderation—some of which might differ or might conflict—that becomes a complete disaster," says Jeff Kosseff, a cybersecurity law professor at the US Naval Academy.

Quoted in Rebecca Kern, "Push to Rein In Social Media Sweeps the States," Politico, July 1, 2022. www.politico.com.

revise Section 230 of the Communications Decency Act to make tech companies take more responsibility for the content on their platforms. One suggested reform would require social media companies to clearly explain how their algorithms promote content on their sites. If they do not, they would not be able to claim legal protections and could be sued for content posted on their sites. Other suggestions include removing legal protections for certain types of content such as hate speech or disinformation.

Frances Haugen, a former Facebook product manager, testified before Congress in 2021 about the social media platform's practices and the need for regulation. In her testimony Haugen urged lawmakers to reform Section 230 to make Facebook responsible for the algorithms it uses to rank content in users' feeds. This reform would force the company to abandon engagement-based ranking, which contributes to promoting misinformation, inflammatory language, and other false content to users. Facebook, she testified, has "100% control over their algorithms. And Facebook should not get a free pass on choices it makes to prioritize growth, virality and reactiveness, over public safety."[33]

However, many people fear that legislation to stop misinformation may go too far and simultaneously sacrifice long-held American rights, including the right to freedom of expression. Since the country's founding, American law and culture have strongly opposed the government regulating speech. The First Amendment to the US Constitution establishes solid protections for these freedoms. "Regulations of social media companies might either indirectly restrict individual speech or directly limit a right to curate an internet platform. . . . Preventing harms caused by 'fake news' or 'hate speech' lies well beyond the jurisdiction of the government,"[34] says John Samples, a vice president at the Cato Institute, a libertarian public policy think tank.

"Preventing harms caused by 'fake news' or 'hate speech' lies well beyond the jurisdiction of the government."[34]

—John Samples, a vice president at the Cato Institute, a public policy think tank

Regulation Worldwide

Other countries are not waiting for the United States to act. They have passed laws that allow government authorities to regulate online content deemed dangerous or false. In December 2021, for example, Greece adopted a law that allows the government to prosecute anyone who spreads false information about the COVID-19 pandemic. Those guilty of spreading false public health information could be sentenced to up to five years in prison. In Singapore a 2019 law grants government authorities the power to determine what is fake news and the power to order online platforms to remove content if it is against the public interest. The definition of what is against the public interest is broad. It includes threats to national security and election integrity and content that damages the public view of the government. In Germany a 2017 law gave social media platforms twenty-four hours to remove posts reported by users as containing fake information or hate speech. Failure to do so could result in fines of up to $52 million.

Even when well-intentioned, these laws are difficult to implement and enforce. In particular, the risk of blocking legitimate content is high. Journalists in Germany expressed concerns about this very problem. According to the journalists, the definition of illegal content is vague under the law. This puts the burden on the platforms to decide what content is illegal. The risk of fines, however, means that social media platforms are more likely to err on the side of removing content that should not have been removed. And this, the journalists contend, is not in the public interest.

Tools for Censorship

Laws that attempt to limit misinformation and disinformation online have many critics. Authoritarian governments can (and do) use these laws to censor speech and ideas they do not like. Scott Griffen, deputy director of the International Press Institute, says:

> While combating online disinformation is a legitimate objective in general, handing governments and state-controlled regulators the power to decide what information is true and what is false is a dangerously wrong path. This is especially the case when this power has no expiration date, as is the case with many of the "fake news" measures introduced under the pandemic. In the wrong hands, like openly authoritarian states, these "fake news" laws are an obvious tool of repression.[35]

Russia provides one example. A 2020 law allows the government to decide what information is true and what is false. Then it can fine media outlets that it says are deliberately spreading false information. Fines can go as high as $123,000. Officials can also

Russian president Vladimir Putin speaks with reporters in December 2020. Russia has a law that allows the government to decide what information is true and what is false. The Russian government has used the law multiple times to block, censor, or fine online media platforms.

block websites that do not remove information deemed to be false when requested. They can also censor sites labeled by the government as disrespectful to the country.

The Russian government has used the power granted it under the law multiple times. Russia's media regulatory agency blocked, censored, and fined online media platforms that were critical of the nation's response to the pandemic. The editor of one website was fined more than $900 for reporting that one thousand graves had been dug for potential pandemic victims. Another journalist was fined almost $500 for interviewing a health care worker who described the difficulties and ventilator shortages Russian doctors and hospitals were facing. According to Galina Arapova, director of the Mass Media Defence Centre in Russia, the government targeted journal-

"While combating online disinformation is a legitimate objective in general, handing governments and state-controlled regulators the power to decide what information is true and what is false is a dangerously wrong path."[35]

—Scott Griffen, deputy director of the International Press Institute

Reporting Hateful Content

Several states have proposed or passed laws that require social media platforms to design a mechanism for users to report hateful content. One such law, passed in New York in June 2022, defines "hateful conduct" as using social media to "vilify, humiliate, or incite violence against a group or a class of persons" based on race and other characteristics. The law requires social media platforms to make it possible for users to report hate speech on their sites. It also requires the companies to respond directly to anyone who reports hate speech. If they do not comply, companies can be fined up to $1,000 per day. A similar bill being considered in New York would require social media companies to provide users a way to report misinformation.

Critics say the New York law defines "hateful conduct" too broadly. They argue that this will allow social media platforms to block speech that is protected by the Constitution. The same concern exists in connection with the proposed law that allows users to report misinformation.

Quoted in Rebecca Kern, "Push to Rein In Social Media Sweeps the States," Politico, July 1, 2022. www.politico.com.

ists who worked for independent media outlets. "In the early stages of the pandemic Russian authorities were enthusiastic about opening cases in an attempt to suppress critical reporting as a way to suppress dissent more widely. But the law has also been worded so vaguely that it can be used against journalists in the future. In that sense, it's really the ace in the deck for the Russian government,"[36] she says.

Stifling Criticism and Dissent

Using these laws, authoritarian governments can accuse critics of spreading false information and prosecute them for legitimate dissent. In Egypt journalist Mohamed Monir was arrested in 2020 for writing an article criticizing the government's response to the COVID-19 pandemic. The government arrested Monir and charged him with spreading false news, misusing social media, and joining a terrorist group. Monir was sent to pretrial detention in a Cairo prison, where he contracted COVID-19. A few weeks later, he died in a hospital isolation unit.

In 2020 Hungary passed legislation allowing the government to fine and jail anyone guilty of spreading misinformation about the COVID-19 pandemic. Critics say Hungarian prime minister Viktor Orbán and his ruling party have long tried to undermine the credibility of journalists by accusing them of publishing fake news. The new law already has a censoring effect in Hungarian newsrooms because people fear punishment for what they say. "The most obvious effect was the wariness of the potential sources—journalists could hardly find sources in the health care system or education system who were willing to talk. There is a definite fear among ordinary people from the consequences of leaking,"[37] says Ágnes Urbán, head of the Mertek Media Monitor think tank in Hungary.

Part of a Complex Solution

Misinformation and disinformation are increasingly complex problems for countries worldwide. The online platforms where misinformation and disinformation circulate have been unable to significantly and consistently slow their spread. And in some cases, they may even have an incentive to let false information continue to circulate. Therefore, many believe that an effective solution must include government legislation and oversight that forces these companies to be accountable for what is posted on their sites.

CHAPTER FOUR

Improving Media and Digital Literacy

Technology and laws might help reduce the amount of false information that circulates online, but they cannot solve the entire problem. Individuals must learn to recognize misinformation and disinformation. "For too long, too many resources and debates have focused on changing the technology, not educating people," say Kristin M. Lord and Katya Vogt of the nonprofit education and development organization IREX. "This emphasis on the supply side of the problem without a similar investment in the demand side may be a less effective use of time and energy. . . . We need to invest more into human-centered solutions focused on improving people's media and information literacy."[38]

What Is Media Literacy?

Media literacy is the ability to use critical-thinking skills to assess and understand information found in newspapers, radio, television, and, especially, on the internet. It helps individuals choose what to read, listen to, and watch and what sources to trust. Media literacy enables people to more easily recognize the media's influence and become more informed and thoughtful media consumers.

With the wealth of information available online, digital literacy has become an essential skill. Online content can be published or shared by anyone, with many motivations. When people are digitally literate, they are much more likely to be able to critically assess the information they find online, determine whether it comes from a source that can be trusted, and make informed decisions about sharing the information with others.

Research has shown media literacy skills consistently help people when they encounter misinformation online. These skills prompt people to ask questions about where information comes from, evaluate its credibility, and better understand the motivations of sources. In a study published in 2020, researchers assessed the effect of a media literacy campaign on a group of American adults. The campaign shared tips on how to spot false news and information online. It gave participants simple rules to help them evaluate the credibility of sources and identify warning signs of potential problem content without requiring a lot of time or effort. The researchers found that participants exposed to the media literacy campaign improved 26.5 percent in their ability to tell the difference between fabricated stories and real ones. "We find that a simple, scalable media literacy intervention can decrease the perceived accuracy of false news content and help people to better distinguish it from factual mainstream news," the researchers wrote. "Our results further suggest that media literacy campaigns could be an effective strategy to help counter false or misleading news, a finding with important real-world implications."[39]

Lacking the Necessary Skills

Media literacy skills can be a critical part of any solution for misinformation and disinformation. However, many people lack the skills and knowledge to assess the information they find online. In a 2022 survey from the public policy initiative Media Literacy Now, only 38 percent of adult participants reported that they had

The wealth of information available to students online means that digital literacy has become an essential skill.

learned how to analyze media messages and content. Erin McNeill, founder and president of Media Literacy Now, says:

> It's clear from this survey that Americans are lacking key life skills they need to navigate an increasingly complex media environment. Policy makers must take note and prioritize media literacy education for all students. . . . People need to understand media systems and have an opportunity to develop skills to analyze messages and think critically about the source and who benefits from messages shared so they can make decisions for themselves and their families, without undue influence and manipulation.[40]

Although today's students are often called digital natives because they have never lived without digital technology, studies show that many students also lack essential media literacy skills. This was the finding of a 2019 Stanford University study of 3,446 high school students from fourteen states. Students taking part in the study completed six media literary exercises. These exercises were used to assess their ability to evaluate online information. More than half (52 percent) believed that a grainy video claiming to show ballot stuffing was strong evidence of US voter fraud, even though the video was filmed in Russia. Two-thirds of students could not tell the difference between actual news articles and ads labeled "sponsored content." And 96 percent of students did not understand why a climate change website with ties to the fossil fuel industry might affect the website's credibility.

Many teachers are not surprised that students lack media literacy skills. According to New York City high school history teacher Amy Berman, battling misinformation in the classroom is an everyday struggle. "We're constantly worried that students aren't savvy enough about the sources they're reading. Or they skip the source altogether. I know it's so pervasive. They see this stuff, and they're susceptible to believing it,"[41] she says.

> "We're constantly worried that students aren't savvy enough about the sources they're reading. Or they skip the source altogether. I know it's so pervasive. They see this stuff, and they're susceptible to believing it."[41]
>
> —Amy Berman, New York City high school history teacher

Media Literacy in Schools

To address the problem, some schools have implemented media literacy programs to teach students how to navigate misinformation and disinformation online. They are teaching students that just because a story spreads widely on the internet—goes viral—does not mean it is true and that content can be made up or manipulated. Students also learn that websites with a ".org" domain name are not always trustworthy or unbiased.

At Palmer High School in Colorado Springs, Colorado, students in history classes are learning how to defend themselves against misinformation. The students spend up to two weeks during the school year learning how false information, bias, and opinionated content can appear across the internet. They practice evaluating sources and tracing the origins of documents. They learn to fact-check and verify websites by researching them on other sites. Students are also learning to critically evaluate the claims made by social media influencers. "With students and adults alike, it's just easy to look at stuff on social media and take it as it is and not question it. It can be difficult to push through that apathy, but it's well worth trying,"[42] says Paul Blakesley, a teacher at Palmer High School who has taught media and information literacy to students for several years.

In 2021 Illinois became the first state to pass legislation that requires public schools to include a unit of media literacy instruction in the high school curriculum. The new law took effect for the 2022–2023 school year. Most Illinois schools added media literacy work to one or more existing classes. Yonty Friesem, an associate professor of civic media at Columbia College Chicago, helped write the Illinois bill. He explains, "The idea is to teach about asking questions of how is it constructed, this message? Who is behind it? What's going on here? And how does it affect me and society? And what's my role in how I'm using media? So it can be in a science experiment, but it can be also in art. It can be talking about civics in social science class."[43]

To develop its school media literacy curriculum, Illinois ran a pilot program in several schools during the 2021–2022 school year. One pilot group included ninth-grade students at Neuqua High School in Naperville, Illinois. In the Neuqua pilot program, biology and geology teachers included media literacy coursework in their teaching. One technique they used is called lateral reading, which means individuals can use the internet to check the accuracy of the information they see online. In one example, students were asked to assess whether they should trust a website called Food Insight to provide accurate information about caffeine intake. "Because it's a 'dot-org' URL, students often think it means that the site is more trustworthy. But if you leave, and open up a new tab and do that 'lateral reading,' you discover that foodinsight.org is actually supported by big beverage corporations that have a

Students work with a librarian in her Digital Student class at a school in Connecticut in 2017. The class teaches students to recognize false information.

vested interest in caffeine seeming trustworthy,"[44] says Stanford University researcher Joel Breakstone. At the end of the school year, students showed a statistically significant improvement in evaluating online sources.

In states that do not require media literacy education, some schools and teachers have added this instruction on their own. "There are challenges with getting this into schools. But it's a necessity for the way we live today because we're all engaging in this online space, especially youth,"[45] says Jimmeka Anderson, founder of the youth-focused group I AM not the MEdia.

In upstate New York, history teacher Timothy Krueger noticed his students having difficulty evaluating misinformation online. Some students brought up a conspiracy theory that they heard on TikTok that Helen Keller, the renowned deaf and blind author and disability advocate, had faked being blind and deaf.

Pause Before Sharing

As tempting as it is to share content that generates controversy and strong emotions, experts say the best way to slow the spread of misinformation is to simply pause before sharing. Studies show that pausing, even briefly, before sharing online, gives people time to think more critically about the information. They have time to evaluate where it comes from, when it was written, and whether or not it is true. In this way a simple pause before sharing can make a person less likely to share questionable content and spread misinformation.

Others told Krueger they were not getting the COVID-19 vaccine because their parents had told them the shot would make them infertile. In response, Krueger began to add lessons about evaluating evidence and fact-checking into his history curriculum. "We're under attack—it's now such an openly polarized society, where teachers are afraid to talk about hot topics or controversial issues," he says. But he believes that teachers are essential to helping young people evaluate information and think clearly for themselves. "If we want them to be a truly intelligent constituency, we have to start now,"[46] he says.

Not All Programs Are Equal

Not all media literacy programs are equal. Some for-profit online learning companies have developed media literacy programs. Often, these programs are funded by large corporations and do little to teach students to analyze information and ask questions about motivations and biases. "There are a lot of groups that advocate for 'media literacy,' but really what's behind them is corporate dollars, trying to get corporate software and corporate products in the classroom to get students familiarized with them,"[47] says Nolan Higdon, history and media studies lecturer at California State University, East Bay.

Experts say that there are several qualities to look for in a good media literacy program. Ideally, media literacy would be taught before high school, since elementary and middle school students go online and have access to smartphones, tablets, and computers. Good programs start by teaching students how to ask questions about information rather than just consume it. Students also learn how to read laterally and check the accuracy of the information they see online. By high school, students should study how fairness, balance, and bias affect online content. By learning these skills, students can better understand the impact of the content they create and learn how to critically evaluate the content they consume.

At Hampton Bays High School on Long Island, New York, social studies students use different news sources to examine current events each week. Social studies teacher Rachel Kelsh discusses the stories with students and explains why some are reliable while others are not. She also teaches students about echo chambers, the term used to describe how some people get news only from sources that reflect their beliefs. Her students learn how social media algorithms promote certain types of content to users. Kelsh believes her students are learning skills they can use whenever they see online content.

Education for All Ages

Young people are not the only ones who would benefit from media literacy education. Surveys show that older Americans also have difficulty differentiating between fact and opinion. This can be seen in a 2018 Pew Research Center survey. That survey asked participants to classify five factual statements and five opinion statements. Overall, about one-fourth (26 percent) of the adult participants were able to classify all five factual statements correctly. Analyzing the results by age group, 32 percent of adults ages eighteen to forty-nine were able to accurately identify the five factual statements, compared to about 20 percent of participants ages fifty and older. For the opinion statements, 35 percent of the adult participants correctly identified all five opinion statements. A similar gap appeared, however, when looking at the results by age

Truth Decay

Americans today seem unable to agree on objective facts. Experts at the nonprofit think tank RAND Corporation say this is a sign that America is experiencing an era of "truth decay." Truth decay has several characteristics, including increasing disagreement about facts, blurring lines between fact and opinion, increasing influence of opinion over facts, and declining trust in factual sources. A large part of the blame, the RAND experts believe, lies with widespread misinformation on social media platforms and some online news sources. Widespread education and media literacy tools can counter truth decay, but only if public officials, tech companies, the media, educators, and individual users work together toward that goal.

group, with 44 percent of the younger group correctly identifying the opinion statements, while only 26 percent of the older group did so.

Older Americans are also more likely to repost and share misinformation. A study by researchers from Princeton University and New York University published in 2019 in *Science Advances* found that adults ages sixty-five and older on Facebook posted seven times as many articles from fake news websites as adults ages twenty-nine and younger.

People of all ages need media literacy education, and some programs are rolling out new tools and programs for people of every age. The News Literacy Project (NLP) has created a mobile app, Informable, that trains users of all ages to spot misinformation through games that improve their fact-checking and news literacy skills. NLP's other tools include a weekly newsletter that offers lessons based on real-world examples of misinformation. "Unless we give the public the tools to be more discerning consumers and sharers of news and information, we're not going to be able to address the misinformation pandemic that threatens to undermine

"Unless we give the public the tools to be more discerning consumers and sharers of news and information, we're not going to be able to address the misinformation pandemic that threatens to undermine the country's civic life and our democracy."[48]

—Alan Miller, founder and CEO of the News Literacy Project

the country's civic life and our democracy,"[48] says NLP founder Alan Miller.

Education Does Not Stop the Spread

Media literacy education gives people the tools to spot false information, but it does not keep them from spreading it online. This was the finding of a 2022 MIT study. According to that study, digital literacy did not lead to greater caution when it comes to sharing information on social media. "While digital literacy was associated with a better ability to identify true versus false information, this did not appear to translate into sharing better-quality information,"[49] write the researchers.

In the study, the MIT researchers showed participants true and false social media posts about politics and COVID-19. To assess their digital literacy, participants were tested on their familiarity with internet-related terms. They were also rated on how they felt about technology and how much they knew about how social media platforms promote content. Participants were also tested

Experts note that even though media literacy gives people the skills to spot misinformation, that does not prevent them from spreading it online.

on critical-thinking skills and how much they knew about the news industry. Then participants were randomly assigned to two groups. One group was asked to assess the accuracy of a set of headlines, while the other group indicated how likely they were to share the headline on social media. Participants with strong digital literacy skills were more likely to identify true headlines accurately. However, they were just as likely to share false information as participants with low digital literacy skills. "If they fail to even consider whether a piece of news is accurate before deciding to share it, their higher ability to identify which news is accurate will be of little assistance,"[50] the researchers write.

The researchers offer one potential explanation for the contradictory results. In prior studies, they noted that most people can become easily distracted on social media. Scrolling quickly through social media feeds and skimming over a tremendous amount of content can cause users to share content without thinking about or evaluating the stories they are sharing.

Everyone's Responsibility

Stopping online misinformation is everyone's responsibility. While technological solutions and new laws may make identifying and removing false content more manageable, the ultimate responsibility to prevent the spread sits with individuals. Experts say that media literacy is an essential skill and will only become more important in the future. In its 2019 report, the nonprofit free speech organization PEN America wrote:

> [Media] literacy is not only society's best defense against the scourge of fraudulent news, but it is also the most effective way to maintain a shared, truth-based foundation of civic discourse while upholding our cherished commitment to protecting freedom of expression within the public square. Ultimately, the most effective, proactive tactic against fraudulent news is a citizenry that is well-equipped to detect and reject fraudulent claims.[51]

SOURCE NOTES

Introduction: Misinformation Goes Viral

1. Quoted in Dan Diamond and Lena H. Sun, "False Claim That CDC Would Require Covid Vaccines for Kids Spurs Outrage," *Washington Post*, October 19, 2022. www.washingtonpost.com.
2. Quoted in Diamond and Sun, "False Claim That CDC Would Require Covid Vaccines for Kids Spurs Outrage."
3. Quoted in Diamond and Sun, "False Claim That CDC Would Require Covid Vaccines for Kids Spurs Outrage."
4. Quoted in Yahoo! News, "Social Media, Free Speech, and Misinformation: Katie Couric Discusses," February 17, 2022. https://news.yahoo.com.

Chapter One: The Problem of Online Disinformation and Misinformation

5. Quoted in Shara Tibken, "5G Has No Link to COVID-19 but False Conspiracy Theories Persist," CNET, October 30, 2021. www.cnet.com.
6. Quoted in Tibken, "5G Has No Link to COVID-19 but False Conspiracy Theories Persist."
7. Quoted in Tibken, "5G Has No Link to COVID-19 but False Conspiracy Theories Persist."
8. Quoted in Mary Blankenship and Aloysius Uche Ordu, "Russia's Narratives About Its Invasion of Ukraine Are Lingering in Africa," *Africa in Focus* (blog), Brookings Institution, June 27, 2022. www.brookings.edu.
9. Quoted in David Klepper, "Experts: Russia Finding New Ways to Spread Propaganda Videos," AP News, October 5, 2022. https://apnews.com.
10. Quoted in Marcus Woo, "How Online Misinformation Spreads," Knowable Magazine, February 11, 2021. https://knowablemagazine.org.

11. Naveena Srinivas, "Can Technology Help Us Solve the Case of Misinformation?," *Insights* (blog), ManageEngine, January 28, 2022. https://insights.manageengine.com.
12. Quoted in Woo, "How Online Misinformation Spreads."
13. Quoted in Jeff Grabmeier, "How Social Media Makes It Difficult to Identify Real News," Ohio State News, March 30, 2020. https://news.osu.edu.
14. Quoted in Katherine Ognyanova et al., "Misinformation in Action: Fake News Exposure Is Linked to Lower Trust in Media, Higher Trust in Government When Your Side Is in Power," Harvard Kennedy School Misinformation Review, June 2, 2020. https://misinforeview.hks.harvard.edu.
15. Quoted in Woo, "How Online Misinformation Spreads."

Chapter Two: Using Technology to Detect Misinformation and Disinformation

16. Gary Fowler, "Fake News, Its Impact and How Tech Can Combat Misinformation," *Forbes*, August 22, 2022. www.forbes.com.
17. Fowler, "Fake News, Its Impact and How Tech Can Combat Misinformation."
18. Fowler, "Fake News, Its Impact and How Tech Can Combat Misinformation."
19. Quoted in Anya Schiffrin et al., "AI Startups and the Fight Against Mis/Disinformation Online: An Update," German Marshall Fund, July 26, 2022. www.gmfus.org.
20. Quoted in Brian T. Horowitz, "Can AI Stop People from Believing Fake News?," *IEEE Spectrum*, March 15, 2021. https://spectrum.ieee.org.
21. Quoted in Iryna Somer, "Lithuanians Create Artificial Intelligence with Ability to Identify Fake News in 2 Minutes," *Kyiv Post* (Kyiv, Ukraine), September 21, 2018. www.kyivpost.com.
22. Quoted in Benjamin Powers, "How the Internet Is Training AI to Make Better Disinformation," Grid, January 26, 2022. www.grid.news.
23. Quoted in Powers, "How the Internet Is Training AI to Make Better Disinformation."
24. Eileen Donahoe, "System Rivalry: How Democracies Must Compete with Digital Authoritarians," Just Security, September 27, 2021. www.justsecurity.org.

25. Quoted in Pooja Reddy, "Could We Fight Misinformation with Blockchain Technology?," *New York Times*, July 6, 2020. www.nytimes.com.
26. Quoted in Reddy, "Could We Fight Misinformation with Blockchain Technology?"
27. Bernard Marr, "Fake News Is Rampant, Here Is How Artificial Intelligence Can Help," Bernard Marr & Co., 2021. https://bernardmarr.com.

Chapter Three: New Laws and Regulations

28. Quoted in Ryan McCarthy, "'Outright Lies': Voting Misinformation Flourishes on Facebook," ProPublica, July 16, 2020. www.propublica.org.
29. Quoted in Kellogg Insight, "Why Are Social Media Platforms Still So Bad at Combating Misinformation?," August 3, 2020. https://insight.kellogg.northwestern.edu.
30. Quoted in Kellogg Insight, "Why Are Social Media Platforms Still So Bad at Combating Misinformation?"
31. Frank Pallone Jr., "Committee on Energy and Commerce Opening Statement as Prepared for Delivery of Chairman Frank Pallone, Jr.," House Committee on Energy and Commerce, March 25, 2021. https://energycommerce.house.gov.
32. Quoted in Christina Pazzanese, "How the Government Can Support a Free Press and Cut Disinformation," *Harvard Gazette*, August 11, 2021. https://news.harvard.edu.
33. Quoted in Marguerite Reardon, "Section 230: How It Shields Facebook and Why Congress Wants Changes," CNET, October 6, 2021. www.cnet.com.
34. John Samples, "Why the Government Should Not Regulate Content Moderation of Social Media," Cato Institute, April 9, 2019. www.cato.org.
35. Quoted in International Press Institute, "Rush to Pass 'Fake News' Laws During COVID-19 Intensifying Global Media Freedom Challenges," October 3, 2020. https://ipi.media.
36. Quoted in International Press Institute, "Rush to Pass 'Fake News' Laws During COVID-19 Intensifying Global Media Freedom Challenges."
37. Quoted in International Press Institute, "Rush to Pass 'Fake News' Laws During COVID-19 Intensifying Global Media Freedom Challenges."

Chapter Four: Improving Media and Digital Literacy

38. Kristin M. Lord and Katya Vogt, “Strengthen Media Literacy to Win the Fight Against Misinformation,” *Stanford Social Innovation Review*, March 18, 2021. https://ssir.org.
39. Andrew M. Guess et al., “A Digital Media Literacy Intervention Increases Discernment Between Mainstream and False News in the United States and India,” *PNAS*, June 22, 2020. www.pnas.org.
40. Quoted in Media Literacy Now, “National Survey Finds Most U.S. Adults Have Not Had Media Literacy Education in High School,” 2022. https://medialiteracynow.org.
41. Quoted in Holly Korbey, “In the Era of Fake News, Teaching Media Literacy Is a Must,” Let Grow, 2022. https://letgrow.org.
42. Quoted in Tiffany Hsu, “When Teens Find Misinformation, These Teachers Are Ready,” *New York Times*, September 8, 2022. www.nytimes.com.
43. Quoted in Steve Inskeep, “Illinois Now Requires Media Literacy Instruction in Its High School Curriculum,” *Morning Edition*, NPR, September 14, 2022. www.npr.org.
44. Quoted in Laura Doan, “Illinois High School Students to Receive Media Literacy Instruction This Year,” CBS News, August 22, 2022. www.cbsnews.com.
45. Quoted in Hsu, “When Teens Find Misinformation, These Teachers Are Ready.”
46. Quoted in Hsu, “When Teens Find Misinformation, These Teachers Are Ready.”
47. Quoted in Olivia Riggio, “Not All Media Literacy Programs Are Created Equal—and Most Have Yet to Be Created,” FAIR, December 15, 2020. https://fair.org.
48. Quoted in Eliza Newlin Carney, “Adults May Need Media Literacy Even More than Students,” The Fulcrum, November 25, 2019. https://thefulcrum.us.
49. Quoted in Sara Brown, “Study: Digital Literacy Doesn’t Stop the Spread of Misinformation,” MIT Sloan School of Management, January 5, 2022. https://mitsloan.mit.edu.
50. Quoted in Brown, “Study.”
51. PEN America, *Truth on the Ballot*. New York: PEN America, 2019. https://pen.org.

FOR FURTHER RESEARCH

Books

Kathryn Hulick, *Media Literacy: Information and Disinformation*. San Diego, CA: ReferencePoint, 2022.

Jennifer LaGarde and Darren Hudgins, *Developing Digital Detectives: Essential Lessons for Discerning Fact from Fiction in the "Fake News" Era*. Portland, OR: International Society for Technology in Education, 2021. Kindle.

Michael Miller, *Fake News: Separating Truth from Fiction*. Minneapolis, MN: Twenty-First Century, 2019.

Cindy L. Otis, *True or False: A CIA Analyst's Guide to Spotting Fake News*. New York: Square Fish, 2022.

Barbara Sheen, *The Fake News Crisis: How Misinformation Harms Society*. San Diego, CA: ReferencePoint, 2022.

Seema Yasmin, *What the Fact? Finding the Truth in All the Noise*. New York: Simon & Schuster Books for Young Readers, 2022.

Internet Sources

Ian Fox, "Don't Be Fooled by Fake Screenshots," Poynter, November 21, 2022. www.poynter.org.

International Press Institute, "Rush to Pass 'Fake News' Laws During COVID-19 Intensifying Global Media Freedom Challenges," October 3, 2020. https://ipi.media.

Monmouth University, "Media Literacy & Misinformation: Evaluating Sources," December 15, 2022. https://guides.monmouth.edu.

Steven Lee Myers and Sheera Frenkel, "How Disinformation Splintered and Became More Intractable," *New York Times*, October 20, 2022. www.nytimes.com.

Pew Research Center, "Many Americans Get News on YouTube, Where News Organizations and Independent Producers Thrive Side by Side," September 28, 2020. www.pewresearch.org.

Pew Research Center, "Mixed Views About Social Media Companies Using Algorithms to Find False Information," March 17, 2022. www.pewresearch.org.

Stanford News, "What Stanford Research Reveals About Disinformation and How to Address It," April 13, 2022. www.news.stanford.edu.

Websites

FactCheck.org
www.factcheck.org
A project of the Annenberg Public Policy Center, FactCheck.org is a nonprofit website that aims to reduce the level of deception and confusion in US politics by providing original research on misinformation and hoaxes.

News Literacy Project
https://newslit.org
The News Literacy Project works with educators and journalists to give students the skills they need to discern fact from fiction and to know what to trust.

PolitiFact
www.politifact.com
PolitiFact is a fact-checking website run by the Poynter Institute for Media Studies, a nonprofit journalism school and research organization. It rates the accuracy of claims by elected officials and others on its Truth-O-Meter.

RAND Corporation
www.rand.org
The RAND Corporation is a public policy think tank. Its website has a section called "Countering Truth Decay," which has information, research, and articles about misinformation, disinformation, and truth decay.

INDEX

Note: Boldface page numbers indicate illustrations.

PICTURE CREDITS

Cover: monticello/Shutterstock.com

5: Prostock-studio/Shutterstock.com
9: Jim West/Alamy Stock Photo
11: Drop of Light/Shutterstock.com
18: Photoroyalty/Shutterstock.com
21: Wachiwit/Shutterstock.com
24: Saikat Paul/Shutterstock.com
26: Loic Salan/Shutterstock.com
34: Rawpixel.com/Shutterstock.com
37: Valerio Pucci/Alamy Stock Photo
41: Kremlin Pool/Alamy Stock Photo
46: Blue Titan/Shutterstock.com
49: Associated Press
53: GaudiLab/Shutterstock.com

ABOUT THE AUTHOR

Carla Mooney is the author of many books for young adults and children. She lives in Pittsburgh, Pennsylvania, with her husband and three children.